THE GIRL WHO
HATED BOOKS

by

Manjusha Pawagi

Illustrated by

Leanne Franson

BEYOND
WORDS
Publishing
I N C

Once there was a girl named Meena. If you looked up her name in a book, you would find that it means "fish" in ancient Sanskrit. But Meena didn't know that because she never looked up anything anywhere. She hated to read, and she hated books.

"They're always in the way," she said. And this was true because in her house books were everywhere. Not just on bookshelves and bedside tables where books usually are, but in all sorts of places where books usually aren't.

There were books in dressers and drawers and desks, in closets and cupboards and chests. There were books on the sofa and books on the stairs, books crammed in the fireplace and stacked on the chairs.

Worse still, her parents were always bringing home MORE books. They kept buying books and borrowing books and ordering books from catalogs. They read at breakfast and lunch and dinner. But when they asked Meena if she wanted to read, she would stamp her feet and shout, "I *hate* books!" And when they tried to read out loud to her, she would put her hands over her ears and shout even louder, "I HATE BOOKS!"

There was probably only one person in the world who hated books more than Meena. And that was her cat, Max. A long time ago, when he was just a kitten, an atlas fell on his tail. It bent the tip like a pipe cleaner. Ever since, he's tried to stay on top of the books rather than below them.

One morning, after Meena moved all the books out of the sink to brush her teeth, she went to the kitchen to get breakfast for herself and Max. First she climbed onto a stack of encyclopedias so she could reach the cereal. Then she opened the fridge and moved a pile of magazines to get the milk. She poured some for herself and some for Max.

"Max!" she called. "Breakfast is ready!"

But Max didn't come. She tried again. "Max!" she called. "Breakfast is ready!" He still didn't come.

"Where could he be?" she wondered. She looked in the bathtub and behind the dryer. She looked under the stairs and on top of the clock. She found more books, but she didn't find Max.

Suddenly she heard a loud "Meeeeyooow!" She ran into the dining room and there he was, stuck on top of the tallest stack of books in the house. It was made up of all the books her parents kept buying her and she kept refusing to read. At the bottom were big shiny picture books from when she was a baby. In the middle were alphabet books and nursery rhymes. At the top, right by the ceiling, were fairy tales and adventure stories. They were all covered in dust.

"Don't worry, Max," Meena called up to him. "I'll rescue you!" She started to climb the pile of books. At first it was easy because the picture books had hard covers, and she felt as if she were climbing stairs. But when she reached the paperbacks her foot slipped on a book of poetry. She lost her balance and started to slide.

CRASH! The books went flying. They fell every which way, the bindings cracking open for the very first time, and the pages flipping apart. As they fell, strange things began to happen. People and animals started falling out of the pages and tumbling to the ground. They dropped one on top of the other, scattering the books and toppling the chairs.

There were princes and princesses, fairies and frogs. Then, a wolf and three pigs and a troll on a log. Humpty Dumpty went flying and then broke in half, behind Mother Goose and a purple giraffe. There were elephants, emperors, emus and elves and an assortment of monkeys tangled up in themselves.

But most of all there were rabbits, falling this way and that. Wild rabbits, and white rabbits, and rabbits with hats.

Meena sat there in the middle of it all, too surprised to move. "I thought books were full of words, not rabbits!" she said, as six more came rolling out of a book beside her.

By now, she couldn't recognize the dining room at all. The elephant was balancing on a coffee table juggling the good china plates. The monkeys had torn down the curtains and were using them as capes. And the rabbits were nibbling on the table legs.

"Stop!" cried Meena. "Go back!" But there was so much barking and grunting and thumping going on that no one heard her speak. She grabbed the nearest rabbit and tried to stuff him into a cookbook, but that scared him so much he wriggled out of Meena's grasp and ran away. She opened another book, and four ducks flew out. She slammed it shut again.

"This won't work," said Meena. "I don't know who goes in which book." She thought for a minute. "I know," she said. "I'll go to everyone and ask them where they belong."

She started with one strange creature she didn't recognize at all. "Who are you?" she asked. "A is for Aardvark!" the animal said angrily, and stomped off in search of her Alphabet Book.

She found a wolf sobbing under the dining room table and asked him where he belonged. "I can't remember if I'm from *Little Red Riding Hood* or *The Three Little Pigs*!" he wailed and blew his nose on the table cloth. But Meena couldn't help him because she had never read either story.

Then she had another idea. She picked up the nearest book and began to read aloud. "Once upon a time," Meena began. "In a land far, far away. . . ."

Slowly, the creatures stopped jumping and howling and gibbering and chattering. They crept closer and closer to hear what happened next. Soon they were all sitting in a circle around her, listening to her read.

When Meena reached the top of the second page, the pigs in the circle jumped up. "That's us!" they cried. "That's our page! That's our book!" They leapt up out of the circle, dove into her lap, and disappeared into the book. Meena clapped it shut before they could pop out again.

She grabbed another story. One by one she began reading all her books. And one by one the creatures found out where they belonged.

At last, there was just one little rabbit in a little blue coat left in the room. Meena slowly picked up a book. It was *The Tale of Peter Rabbit*. "Maybe I could keep this rabbit with me," she thought. She was beginning to feel lonely now that everyone else was gone.

But the little rabbit stood in front of her, shifting nervously from foot to foot and twitching his fuzzy nose. He was anxious to get back home. So, with a big sigh, Meena opened the last book. The rabbit hopped in, and with a flash of his white cotton tail, he was gone.

The house was quiet. Max sat on some books washing his face. Meena sighed. "I'll never see those rabbits again!" she said.

Then she noticed that the books were still there, lying around her. She started to smile.

When her parents came in that afternoon they couldn't believe their eyes. Not because the curtains were gone and the dishes were broken and the table legs were chewed up. But because there, sitting in the middle of the room, was Meena. She was reading a book.

For my parents, who love to read. —M.P.
For Marlo, who discovered books despite his bookworm big sister! —L.F.

BEYOND WORDS PUBLISHING, INC.
20827 N.W. Cornell Road, Suite 500
Hillsboro, Oregon 97124-9808
503-531-8700
1-800-284-9673

First Published in Canada by Second Story Press, 1998
This edition published by Beyond Words, 1999
Distributed to the book trade by Publishers Group West

Printed in Hong Kong

Library of Congress Cataloging-in-Publication Data

Pawagi, Manjusha.
The girl who hated books / by Manjusha Pawagi ; illustrated by Leanne Franson.
24 p.   22 cm.
Summary: Although she lives in a house full of avid readers, Meena hates
books—until she discovers the magic inside them.
ISBN 1-58270-006-0 (cloth)
[1. Books and reading—Fiction. 2. Characters in literature-
-Fiction.]   I. Franson, Leanne, ill. II. Title.
PZ7.P1365GI 1999
[E]—DC2198-41606
CIP
AC

The corporate mission statement of Beyond Words Publishing, Inc.: